MW00906221

Let's Play
POP-OUT
Mask Book

Bath · New York · Cologne · Melbourne · Delhi
Hong Kong · Shenzhen · Singapore · Amsterdam

Sofia

Sofia is a big-hearted, kind princess. She's friendly to everyone and tries to help anyone in need. She is very curious and loves to learn new things. Sofia is always ready for an exciting adventure!

Ask an adult to help!

To remove your masks, tear the tabs along the perforations. Then gently press along the fold lines, slip the elastic band over your head, and you'll be ready for some royal fun and games!

Sofia loves to have her friends over to the castle for a tea party. How many teacups do you see?

What are you curious about?

Amber

Amber is a classic princess—she is beautiful and has good manners. Since Sofia came into her life as her stepsister, Amber is learning to loosen up and try new things. She's having more fun than ever before!

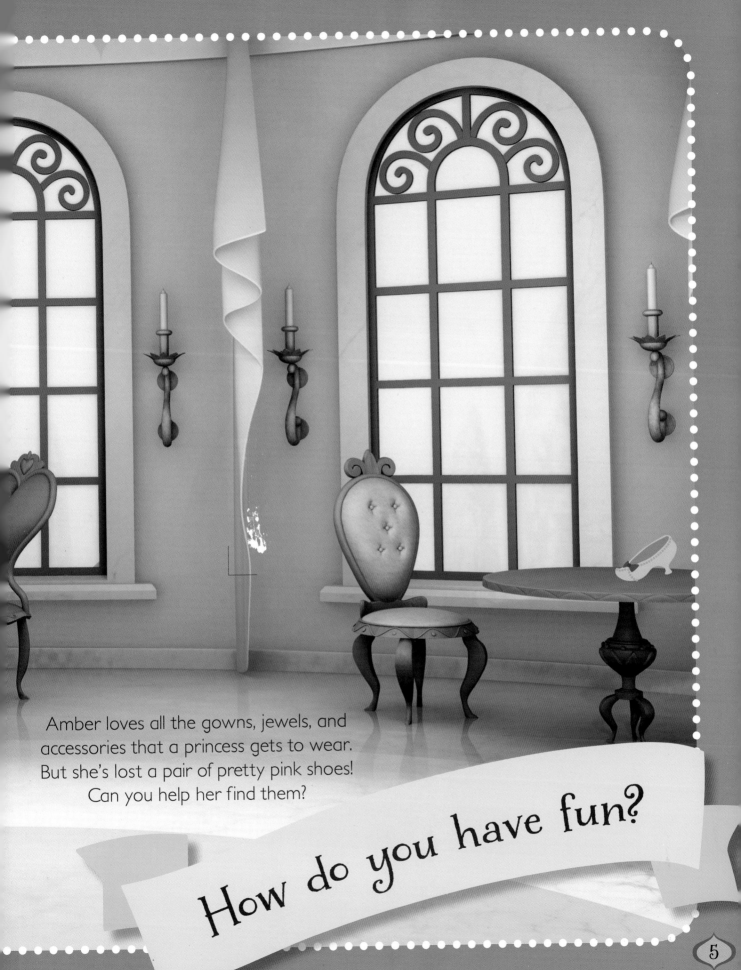

Amber loves all the gowns, jewels, and accessories that a princess gets to wear. But she's lost a pair of pretty pink shoes! Can you help her find them?

How do you have fun?

Clover

Don't ever call Clover cute. And whatever you do, don't try to cuddle with him—at least, not unless you first give him a carrot or something else that's good to eat! This gruff bunny is Sofia's very best friend.

Clover loves to munch on carrots!
How many carrots can you spot?

What is your favorite food?

Whatnaught

This furry little fellow is a good friend to both Clover and Sofia. He never says anything, but he always has a big grin on his face! He's also there to lend a paw whenever help is needed.

Whatnaught is always with one of his friends. When he's not with Clover and Sofia, he's often with Mia or Robin. What kind of animals are they?

Who are your best friends?

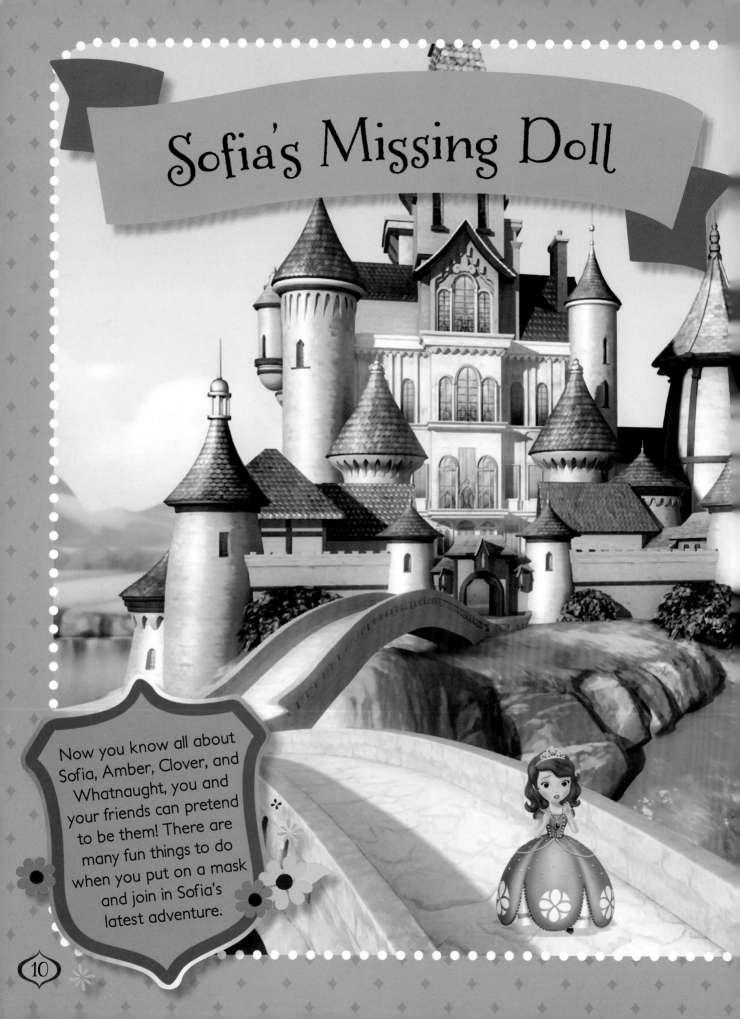

Sofia's Missing Doll

Now you know all about Sofia, Amber, Clover, and Whatnaught, you and your friends can pretend to be them! There are many fun things to do when you put on a mask and join in Sofia's latest adventure.

Sofia's favorite doll is missing!
Can you help her find it?
It must be somewhere in
the castle or the grounds.
Let's start looking!

Join in!

Put on the Sofia mask. Ask an adult
to lend you a necklace that you
can pretend is Sofia's amulet.
Wear something purple, too, if you
can—it's Sofia's favorite color!

Sofia looks around the castle grounds for her doll. She left it under a tree for just a few minutes, and now it has disappeared! In its place is a book with some handwritten pages.

Sofia picks up the book and begins to read aloud from it:

Follow these words, and if you do,
your doll will be returned to you.
First hop around and touch your nose,
then bend down and touch your toes.

"How odd!" says Sofia. But she does what the book says. So do Clover and Whatnaught, who have stopped by to visit.

Join in

Ask a friend to put on the Clover mask, and ask another to put on the Whatnaught mask. See if an adult can make tails for Clover and Whatnaught. Then all three of you should hop around and touch your noses, and your toes!

Do you see someone that Sofia and Amber haven't spotted, hiding behind one of the columns?

"Next the book says to go to the ballroom," Sofia tells Clover and Whatnaught.

On their way to the ballroom, Sofia sees Amber and tells her about the book. Amber is curious, too, so she joins them as Sofia reads the next page:

Round and round you dance.
Leap, hop, skip, and prance!
One, two, three. One, two, three,
I wish my doll would come to me.

The girls dance and say the words over and over.

After a few minutes, Amber stops and pouts. "Oh, this is silly," she says. "How is this going to help you find your doll?"

Join in

Ask a friend to put on the Amber mask. See if an adult can find or make a fan for Amber. Then you and your friend in the Amber mask should dance and repeat the words from the book a few times.

"I don't know," says Sofia. "But figuring it out is half the fun! Come on, we must go to the throne room next."

Sofia explains that they must curtsy, and then she reads the next page aloud:

Give your hair a gentle tug,
then rub your feet on the rug.
Turn around three times and say,
I want my doll back right away!

"I will not tug my hair!" says Amber. But she does the rest along with Sofia, Clover, and Whatnaught.

Do you see James hiding? Sofia has spotted him! Aha! This is one of his practical jokes. Sofia decides to play along because she doesn't want to spoil his fun. There's only one more page in the book.

Join in

Everyone should do their best curtsy and then, except for your friend in the Amber mask, give their hair a gentle tug. All four of you should rub your feet on the floor and turn around three times.

"There's only one page left," says Sofia. "We have to go to my bedroom."

Sofia reads the very last page:

Now it's time to quietly creep,
to the place where you sleep.
Then put this book upon your head,
and take a look beneath your bed!

Sofia places the book on her head and walks carefully toward her bed. Clover, Whatnaught, and Amber follow her.

Join in

Find four books, then you and your friends should each put one on your head. See how far you can walk, without touching the book, before it falls off!

Sofia bends down, looks under her bed, and pulls out her doll. "Hooray!" she shouts, as Clover and Whatnaught clap.

"Surprise!" says James as he comes into Sofia's bedroom.

Amber snaps her fan, stamps her foot, and then laughs. "I should have known it was you!" she says. "After all, the handwriting in that book is terrible!"

Join in

Throw your hands up in the air and shout "Hooray!" Your friends wearing the Clover and Whatnaught masks should clap. Your friend in the Amber mask should snap a pretend fan, stamp her foot, and then laugh.

Let's Pretend Again!

Here are just a few ideas for how you and your friends can pretend to be Sofia and her friends. Why not switch masks this time, so you can each pretend to be someone else?

Hide your favorite doll or stuffed animal somewhere in your room while your three friends close their eyes. Then they should search for it, pretending to look around the castle. Whoever finds the doll first is the next to hide it.

Clover and Whatnaught are hungry! Whoever has the Clover mask should pretend to be pulling up fresh carrots from the castle's vegetable garden to eat. The friend with the Whatnaught mask should search the room as if looking for acorns.

Amber and Sofia love to have sleepover parties at the castle with their friends. Pretend you and your friends are at a sleepover party. Do you want to have a friendly pillow fight?

Sofia's amulet allows her to understand animals when they talk. Pretend you can understand animals, too, and have a conversation with the family pet or with your favorite stuffed animal!

So Long, Sofia!

Thanks for joining Sofia and her friends on their adventure!
They couldn't have found her lost doll without you.
Remember, you and your friends can go on lots of great
adventures, too. All you need is your imagination!